This story is set in New York. I lived there once for a short time and one day, while I was on a train, I saw a man standing on the very top of a high building with a cloud of pigeons whirling around his head. It was an extraordinary sight and I couldn't get it out of my mind. I told everyone about what I'd seen and eventually I came to meet Mike who kept pigeons on the top of a derelict building in New York's Lower East Side. I climbed to the top of Mike's building just once – I wasn't brave enough to do it again! First we climbed three floors using the fire escape. Then we went through a window and across the timbers of a burned-out floor. Out of the window on the other side, we scaled a ladder fixed to the outside wall up to the roof! But when I was up there it was worth it. New York rooftops are truly special places. Some are like gardens. Some are like playgrounds and children write their "tag" and street addresses on their chimney-pots so their friends on other rooftops can see where they live. And some people, like Mike, keep homing pigeons on them.

From the giddy height of Mike's rooftop I wondered what I would see if I could fly over New York. I wondered about homes in the sky. And so I came to make this book.

For Andrew in admiration

This edition published 2001 by Walker Books Ltd, 87 Vauxhall Walk, London SE11 5HJ

10 9 8 7 6 5 4 3 2 1

© Jeannie Baker 1984, 2001

This book has been typeset in Souvenir Demi-Bold

Printed in Hong Kong

British Library Cataloguing in Publication Data:
a catalogue record for this book is available from the British Library

ISBN 0-7445-7585-0

HOME
IN THE
SKY

Jeannie Baker

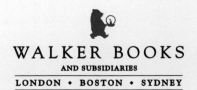

WALKER BOOKS
AND SUBSIDIARIES
LONDON • BOSTON • SYDNEY

Every day, at sunrise and sunset,
a flock of pigeons bursts into the sky.

The pigeons belong to Mike.
They live on the roof
of an abandoned, burned-out building.
Mike's dog, Werewolf, lives on the third floor,
and guards the pigeons
when Mike is not there.

Every morning, before feeding time,
Mike lets the pigeons out of their coop.
They fly in a swirling cloud
across the rooftops.
When Mike whistles, the pigeons know
it is time to come back for breakfast
and they fly home.

But one morning when Mike whistles
one of his pigeons flies away.

Where are you going, Light?

Light flies and flies but he's hungry.
He's missed his breakfast.
Light lands on the ground and tries to share
the scraps some street pigeons have found.
But the street pigeons screech and peck,
and snatch the food from him.

Light flies on…
It starts to rain.
His wings become heavy.

Where will you go now, Light?

Light flies through an open doorway.
Shelter!
Swish, the doors close behind him.

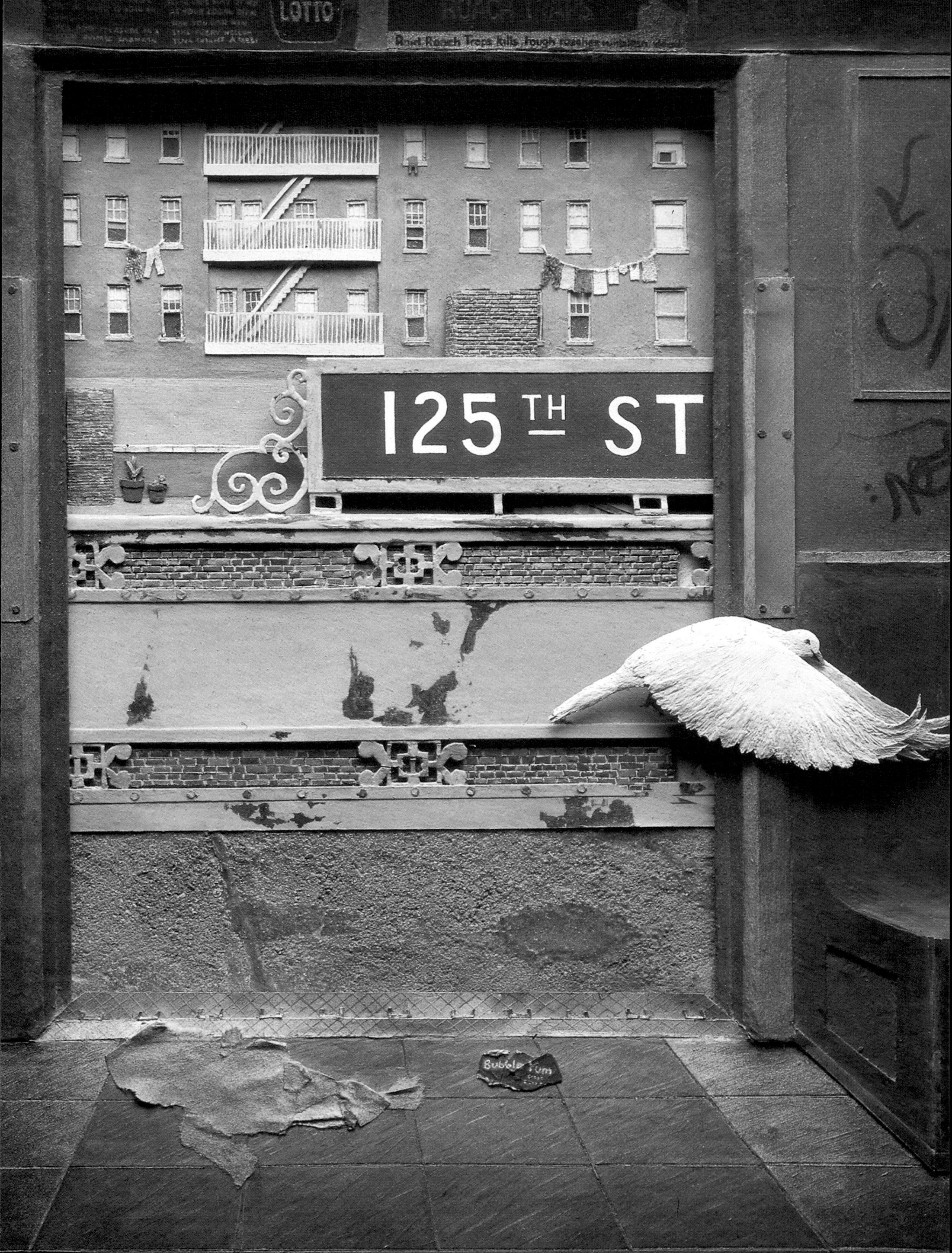
LOTTO
125TH ST
Bubble Yum

A boy picks him up. He holds Light firmly, and gently strokes his feathers so Light feels safe.

The boy walks home
cuddling Light to his chest.

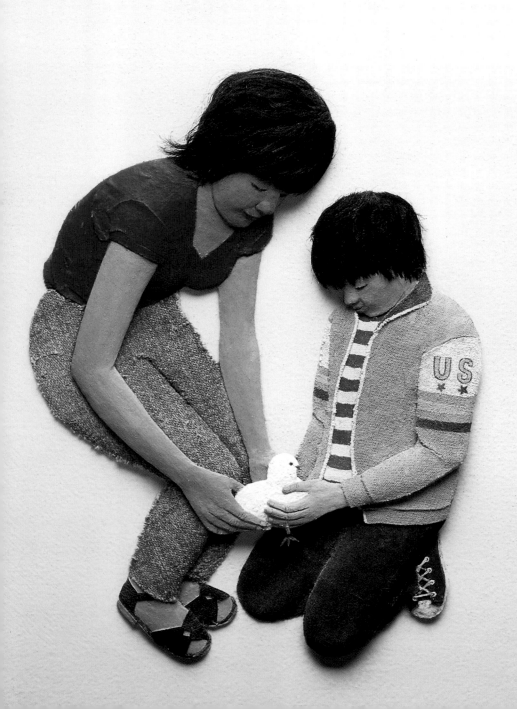

"Can I keep him?" he asks his mother.
"But Carlos, he already has a home," she says,
and explains that the band around Light's leg
means he belongs to someone.

Carlos takes Light to the window
and places him gently on the sill.
He hopes Light will want to stay.
But Light spreads his wings
and flies away.

Where will you go now, Light?

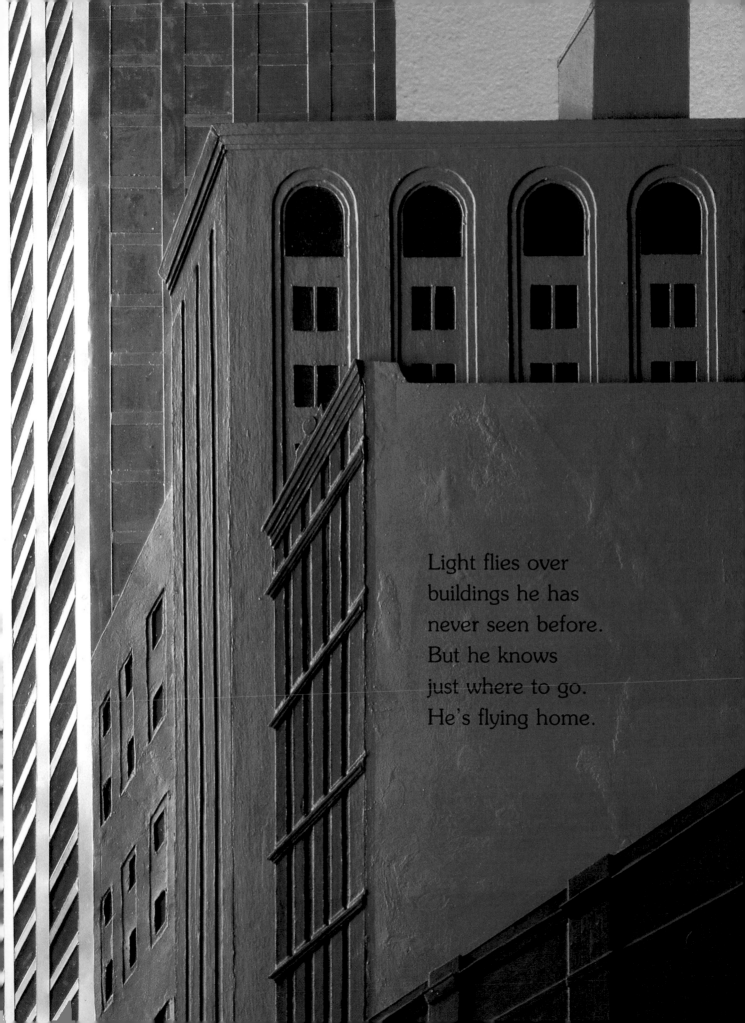

Light flies over
buildings he has
never seen before.
But he knows
just where to go.
He's flying home.

That evening,
as Mike feeds his pigeons,
someone lands on his shoulder,
someone nestles against his face.
"Welcome home," says Mike.
"Where did you go?"

Next morning, from his own rooftop,
Carlos sees a flock of pigeons
sweeping across the sky.
He is sure he sees one white pigeon among them.
He is sure he sees Light
at home in the sky.

How This Book Was Made

All the pictures in this book are collage constructions. Altogether they took me about two years to make. I started by collecting grasses, leaves, pigeon feathers and any other natural materials that I thought might be useful. I had to treat them to strengthen them and prevent their colours from fading. For example, the grasses and leaves were bleached with chemicals and soaked in glycerine for several days. Then they were sprayed with oil paint chosen to match their natural colour as closely as possible. I used other materials as well. The tree trunks were modelled from clay, fabric was chosen for the clothes and hair was cut for the characters. The miniature newspapers and pieces of litter were all cut out and hand-painted.

About Pigeons

Light is a domestic pigeon. The pigeons he meets in the street and which live in the streets of most cities around the world are feral pigeons. But they are both types of Rock Dove. Domestic pigeons can be trained always to come back to the same place to roost. That's why they are also called homing pigeons. Long ago in Ancient Rome and Ancient Egypt, people kept homing pigeons to carry important messages. The pigeons would be released a long way from home, perhaps in another country, with a message tied to their legs. The pigeons would then fly back to their roosts and the message would be delivered.